MR PATTACAKE

Stephanie Baudet

Sweet Cherry
Publishing

Published by Sweet Cherry Publishing Limited
Unit E, Vulcan Business Complex
Vulcan Road
Leicester, LE5 3EB
United Kingdom

First published in the UK in 2014
ISBN: 978-1-78226-056-1
©Stephanie Baudet 2014
Illustrations ©Creative Books
Illustrated by Ojoswi Sur & Joy Das

Mr Pattacake and the Big Idea

Printed in India by Ajanta Offset and Packagings Limited

Pattacake, Pattacake, baker's man,
Bake me a cake as fast as you can;
Pat it and prick it and mark it with P,
Put it in the oven for you and for me.

Pattacake, Pattacake, baker's man,
Bake me a cake as fast as you can;
Roll it up, roll it up;
And throw it in a pan!

Pattacake, Pattacake, baker's man.

MR PATTACAKE
and the
BIG IDEA

Mr Pattacake picked up the envelope off the mat and opened it, peering closely at the writing. His eyes widened and he smiled a big smile.

'Yippee!' he shouted.

He then did a silly little dance on the spot. Now, it's not a good idea to do silly dances when holding a mug of tea, and it spilt over the side and slopped over the letter.

'**Oh DRIBBLE !**' said Mr Pattacake. He always said that when he was cross.

His big chef's hat wobbled as he shook the drops of tea off the letter.

'Look at this, Treacle,' he said, showing the letter to his cat, who had nearly jumped out of his skin when Mr Pattacake had shouted.

'I'm in business! I've been asked to make the food for a children's birthday party,' said Mr Pattacake. 'There will be one hundred children!' He waved the letter in the air.

Treacle didn't answer. He was only a cat after all. He did what all cats do. He just went on washing his paw as if he had not heard... But he knew what Mr Pattacake had said. Being in business meant being busy, and in Mr Pattacake's case, that meant busy cooking and baking. Treacle knew there was always something for him to eat when Mr Pattacake was cooking, which was why he had grown into such a big, fat cat.

'I must start planning,' said Mr Pattacake. 'Such a lot of food to make.' He threw the letter onto the worktop where it slowly soaked up a puddle of spilt ketchup.

He then put on his glasses and sat at the table making a list of what he would need. He had to make sure that this was the best party ever for… what was his name? He picked up the letter and wiped off the ketchup with his sleeve so he could read the name. It was for Jack. It was his eighth birthday.

Treacle sat looking up at Mr Pattacake, his ears pricked up, listening intently.

'Right,' said Mr Pattacake. 'We'll make pizzas and monkey tail sandwiches. And we'll have popcorn and crisps and fruit kebabs. And sausages on sticks too.'

Treacle stared hard at Mr Pattacake.

'Oh, of course, Treacle. There are the chocolate mice. I hadn't forgotten.' Mr Pattacake was famous for his chocolate mice.

Treacle seemed to nod slightly.

'So, we'll need…' Mr Pattacake bent over the piece of paper to write.

Ten loaves of bread,

A kilo of chicken,

A thousand mini sausages,

Fruit,

Cream cheese and sultanas,

Lots of drinks and crisps,

Popping corn,

Chocolate for the chocolate mice,

And jelly. Lots and lots of jelly. Children loved jelly and ice-cream.

And then there was the special cake. That was the thing that Mr Pattacake loved doing most. He always tried to make the cake as realistic as possible. This one would need wheels, and he so was going to use *real* ones.

At last the list was finished. Mr Pattacake loved making lists. It was an important part of planning, he always said, and the planning was just as important as the cooking.

Sometimes he even made lists when there *wasn't* a cooking job. There were lists of food that he liked, lists of songs that he whistled whilst he was cooking, and one day, he had even made a list of naughty things that Treacle did – which was the longest list of all! Like when he stayed out playing all night, and when he stole some little sausages Mr Pattacake had just cooked, and hid them under his bed.

On the day of the party Mr Pattacake got up very early and jumped in his little yellow van to buy the food.

There was a lot of it, and he staggered indoors with heavy bags and boxes.

Soon the big fridge in his kitchen was full. A dozen boxes were stacked on the floor and several bulging bags were on the worktops. Some contained fruit – apples, oranges, strawberries and bananas. Then there were boxes of crisps, and sliced bread. Treacle sat on top of a stack of boxes containing the chocolate. He knew what Mr Pattacake would be making first.

The chocolate mice.

And chocolate mice were the next best thing to real mice.

Mr Pattacake got out his biggest pan to melt the chocolate. Soon it was glop-glopping and spitting out little showers of chocolate onto the floor and the worktop.

Treacle was not allowed on the worktop but he *was* allowed on the floor. He licked up the drops of chocolate as they rained down on him, darting from place to place as a new drop fell. Then he sat and washed his whiskers, purring contentedly.

Mr Pattacake poured the chocolate into the mouse moulds and found a space on the worktop for them to set. He put in little silver balls for eyes and stuck a piece of edible string to each one for a tail. One of the tails was a little longer than the rest and hung down over the edge of the worktop.

Later on, when Mr Pattacake was not looking, that particular little mouse escaped. The chef didn't notice. He was busy spreading the slices of bread with two delicious fillings. There was chicken and avocado, and there was cream cheese, carrot and sultanas. He then rolled them up and cut them into round monkey tail sandwiches. He boiled the big kettle to make the jelly, and greased the trays to cook the sausages.

The kitchen was full of steam and he could barely see, so he had to take off his glasses, wipe them with his handkerchief and switch off the kettle. Then he bent down to get his big jelly moulds out of the cupboard. But as he reached out, he clumsily knocked the tray of chocolate mice with his elbow. They all flew into the air, tails waving and silver eyes sparkling.

They tumbled back down, with some landing on the floor and some on the worktop. A few had ears missing and some were smashed into a hundred pieces.

'**Oh DRIBBLE!**' Mr Pattacake sighed. He picked up the mice he could salvage from the ones which had landed on the worktop, pulled off their tails, and popped them back into the pan to melt. He would have to start all over again, but Mr Pattacake was used to things going wrong.

Treacle had watched the mice flying through the air, especially the ones that had flown off the worktop. He had been a very good cat and cleaned the floor up. Not one bit of the chocolate mice was left. He licked his lips and lay on the floor, his tummy full.

Suddenly, Treacle's ears twitched, and he looked towards the window. A dark furry face was peering in.

Treacle was used to children sometimes looking in to see what Mr Pattacake was cooking. Mr Pattacake would always take off his hat and wave it at them, giving them each a piece of a broken chocolate mouse. (The mice were very accident-prone).

But *children* did not have furry faces. Treacle's fur stood on end and he made a horrible yowling noise.

'Be quiet, Treacle. I'm trying to think,' said the chef. But Treacle jumped onto the worktop (where he was not allowed) and stared out of the window, nose to nose with the black furry face outside. It was lucky that there was a pane of glass between them; he might not have been so brave had it not been there. Tortoiseshell cats could be very fierce, you see.

He yowled again, and this time Mr Pattacake looked up. 'Who is it, Treacle?' He walked over to the window to have a look. 'Well, I might have known. It's that mischievous cat, Naughty Tortie! She always seems to know when I'm baking.' He banged on the window at her. 'Shoo!'

But Naughty Tortie was not going to go that easily. Why should Treacle have all that lovely food which found its way onto the floor? She jumped back onto the ground and slunk round the side of the house, waiting for her opportunity.

As Mr Pattacake was pouring boiling water onto the jellies, the doorbell rang. It was the lady whose little boy was having the party.

'Come in!' said Mr Pattacake.

'All that food for just ten children?' she said, coming into the kitchen and looking at the mountain of sandwiches and plates of fairy cakes.

'Ten?' said Mr Pattacake. 'But your letter said a hundred.'

She shook her head. 'Ten children will be difficult enough. The entertainer is ill and I can't get anyone else at such short notice. I don't know what we are going to do. I came to ask if you knew any party entertainers.'

Mr Pattacake didn't. Except for Treacle that is. Treacle had his little act, but that was best left as a secret for now. No one would believe it unless they saw it. All he could think about were the hundreds of sandwiches, the thousand mini sausages, and all the rest of the food. How he hated wasted food!

'I don't know what we're going to do, Mr Pattacake,' said Jack's mother. '*Please* try to think of something.'

When she had gone, Mr Pattacake went to read the letter again, but the ketchup had smudged the ink. He was *sure* it had said one hundred children. Had he been wearing his glasses when he read it?

'Now, Treacle,' he said, wiping his brow with a handkerchief and opening the window for some fresh air. 'What are we going to do with all this food?'

Treacle would have normally had the answer to that question, but right now he did not want to think about it. He had eaten too many bits of chocolate mouse. So instead he just lay on the floor in a patch of sunlight, his eyes half closed, feeling slightly sick.

'You've eaten too much, haven't you?' Mr Pattacake said. 'Chocolate isn't good for cats. Now, where was I? Ah, I was making the jellies.'

As he stared at the giant jelly moulds, he had an idea.

After he'd put the popping corn in the pan to pop, he went out of the door and into his garage.

Lying against one wall was the new rigid pond liner which he was going to use to make a lovely pond in the garden when he had the time. It was a very big pond liner.

Mr Pattacake took off the plastic wrapping and smiled happily. His idea would at least solve one problem. He went back to his kitchen. While he was out in the garage, he had left Treacle in charge. That may not have been a good idea, although he knew Treacle had had enough to eat, so he would not steal any food.

However, he had forgotten about Naughty Tortie.

The tortoiseshell cat had seen her chance and sneaked in through the open window. Mr Pattacake looked at the mess with dismay. On the worktop the monkey tail sandwiches had been torn apart and all the chicken and cream cheese licked away, leaving bits of bread scattered everywhere. A carton of milk had been knocked over and was gently glug-glugging over the big plate of fairy cakes, which were turning to mush.

Mr Pattacake was speechless and his big chef's hat wobbled wildly.

'**OH DRIBBLE !**' he said. 'Treacle! Where are you?'

The big ginger cat crept out of a cupboard, where he'd been hiding. He looked ashamed of himself and could barely look Mr Pattacake in the eye.

But secretly, Mr Pattacake knew that Treacle was no match for Naughty Tortie, especially when he had eaten so much. Naughty Tortie, on the other hand, could be loving and purry when she wanted, yet turn into a wild animal when the mood took her.

The popping corn was now beginning to sizzle.

Mr Pattacake stepped carefully into the mess, but not carefully enough. His foot slipped on a splodge of cream cheese, and for a moment he slid across the kitchen floor like an ice skater, although not as gracefully.

Then, with a crash, he landed on the floor on his bottom. He narrowly missed Treacle, who had to move quickly, which was quite a struggle, especially after eating all that chocolate.

'Ouch!' said Mr Pattacake, struggling to his feet. 'This is not turning out to be a very good day.'

So as well as having to clean up the mess and make the sandwiches and fairy cakes all over again, (although not as many this time round), Mr Pattacake also created his 𝔹𝕀𝔾 𝕀𝔻𝔼𝔸.

The popping corn was getting hotter, and jiggling in the pan…

There was still the problem of too much food, and Treacle couldn't come up with a single suggestion as to what to do with it, so in the end Mr Pattacake thought of a plan himself, and phoned Jack's mum to explain.

He had just put down the phone, when there was a loud **POP** and then a **CRACK.** Mr Pattacake jumped, and Treacle screeched, shooting out of the cat-flap like a rocket.

They had both forgotten about the corn.

POP! CRACK! BANG!

The mice that had already set landed back on the worktop and broke, but those which were only half set stuck to the ceiling, drooped, and fell onto the floor in chocolaty splodges.

'OH DRIBBLE!' exclaimed Mr Pattacake. He did another silly dance, but this time out of annoyance. More chocolate mice would have to be made.

At two o'clock he loaded all the food into the van as well as the **BIG IDEA** and the birthday cake (including wheels). He then drove slowly through the town with his window open.

'Come to a children's party in the park!' he shouted. 'Free food and drink.'

Treacle was feeling much better, so he sat on the roof, doing what he did best (besides eating). He played a jolly tune on his lute, plucking its many strings delicately.

Whether it was Mr Pattacake's shouting or Treacle playing the lute, the children and their parents soon began to follow the van, running and skipping with excitement, just like when the Pied Piper led all the children out of Hamlyn.

When they reached the park, Mr Pattacake opened the doors of the van and the children crowded round.

'Can I help, Mr Pattacake?' It was Jack, whose birthday it was.

'Mr Pattacake's party in the park,' said Daisy, giggling as she reached out for a bowl of popcorn and took it to a park table.

'With pink popcorn and pizzas,' said Jack, coming back for another plate.

'And me with a black and blue bruised bum,' said Mr Pattacake, recalling how he'd slipped and fallen, and nearly doing a replay in the process.

When it was all laid out, the children ate and drank and played while the mums and dads sat on a bench or on the grass and had a rest. Mr Pattacake just leaned against a tree. (You know why he didn't sit down, don't you?)

Suddenly there was a commotion.

'Mr Pattacake!' Daisy came running towards him. 'Some big girls are stealing our food.'

'They can have some too, Daisy.'

'No, but they're putting packets of crisps in their bags,' Daisy panted, partly from running and partly from outrage.

'And they're throwing popcorn all over the place.'

Mr Pattacake stood up to his full height and adjusted his big chef's hat. Stealing he did not like, but wasted food he absolutely *loathed*. He strode down to where two older girls were stuffing things in a bag, surrounded by the younger children, who were all shouting.

'What's going on?' Mr Pattacake fumed as his big chef's hat wobbled with disapproval. When the girls turned and saw him, they laughed.

'What are you going to do about it?' one of them said. 'It's a free party.'

'You're welcome to eat the food here,' said Mr Pattacake, 'but you're not welcome to take it away or throw it about.'

In response, the other girl picked up a handful of popcorn from a bowl and threw it at him.

The younger children gasped, and there was silence as they watched Mr Pattacake's hat wobble violently, as if he were going to explode. Then some of them glared at the girl standing next to Jack.

'That's your sister, Sara. Why don't you say something?'

'Yes, tell her to stop spoiling our party.'

'She won't take any notice of me,' said Sara.

'Isn't your mum here?' asked Jack.

Sara shook her head. 'No, I came with Daisy's mum.'

The older girls smirked at Mr Pattacake and continued filling their bags.

Suddenly, there was a terrible yowl, which made everyone jump and back away from the source of the noise.

Treacle's fur was standing on end and his tail was fluffed up to twice its normal size. His back was arched and his teeth bared. He yowled again and raised a paw, claws extended. Then he growled and spat and hissed.

The two girls jumped back, eyes wide with fear. Then they dropped their bags and ran, and all the children cheered. They looked down at Treacle, who was now back to his normal size and purring loudly, a big cat's smile on his face.

'Treacle! Treacle!' Jack chanted. Everyone else joined in as well. Mr Pattacake secretly hoped they would stop before Treacle became impossible to live with. He would expect all sorts of extra treats for being the hero of the hour.

Everyone cleared up the leftovers and took them to Mr Pattacake's van. Just before four o'clock, the mums and dads gathered up their tired children and went home, all except for the nine children who had been invited to Jack's party. *They* still had the best part to come. The birthday cake!

While the children went back to Jack's house in their parents' cars, Mr Pattacake and Treacle set off in the van.

Jack's house was on a hill, so Mr Pattacake
made sure the handbrake was on. He didn't want his
van rolling away.

Ten children burst out of the door and ran to meet them.

Ten pairs of eyes watched as he opened the van doors. What was Jack's cake going to be like? They knew that Mr Pattacake had made fairy castles and spaceships, and dragons and witches before. His cakes were legendary.

The **BIG IDEA** was right at the back and out of sight.

Suddenly, there was a rumbling noise and a clatter. Then something rolled out of the van, landed with a crash on the road, and set off rolling down the hill on its real wheels.

It was Jack's cake, shaped like a skateboard.

It took everyone by surprise. They all gasped and watched as it began to roll down the hill. Everyone seemed frozen in shock, and not one of them thought to grab it before it picked up speed.

'My cake!' shouted Jack.

He and Daisy set off after it, followed by the other children. Mr Pattacake was rooted to the spot, his heart thumping. He could only watch as it sped away, knowing he couldn't run fast enough to catch the cake. A cake on wheels (real ones) was very fast indeed.

All that work for nothing. And poor Jack now had no cake, because at the bottom of the hill was the main road. Mr Pattacake felt miserable. He hated it when things went wrong, and they often did.

The children would be smart enough to stop at the main road, but the cake wouldn't. It knew nothing about the dangers of traffic, and besides, it didn't have any brakes.

But Mr Pattacake couldn't just stand there. Even though he had no chance of catching the cake, he had to do something. So he set off after it, behind Jack and his nine friends.

They all hurtled down the hill.

Treacle didn't run. He decided that it was a waste of time and energy, although he could probably run faster than any of them. But it was futile. There was no chance of catching up with a cake which had had a head start.

As he watched the commotion, he saw something run out in front of the cake.

It was Naughty Tortie!

'Watch out, Naughty Tortie!' panted Mr Pattacake. Although the cat was a nuisance, he still didn't want her to get run over by a runaway cake.

Even Treacle was worried. His head was craned forward and he didn't move a whisker.

But Naughty Tortie just stood bravely in the middle of the road right in the path of the cake.

The children stopped, gasping for breath, and watched. Mr Pattacake staggered to a stop. He really needed to save his energy for later.

As the cake hurtled towards her, Naughty Tortie just put out her paw, and stopped the cake in its tracks. Then she stood there, her paw still resting on the skateboard cake.

Naughty Tortie stared at Mr Pattacake and he stared back. He had been around cats long enough to know exactly what they were thinking. The tortoiseshell cat was not going to let them have the cake unless she was invited to the party.

'What do you think, Jack?' said Mr Pattacake.
'Shall we invite her to your party? That's the only way
she will let us have the cake.'

Jack was looking at the cake with disbelief. The journey down the hill had not spoilt it one bit. It was such a realistic cake he could have almost put his foot on it and whizzed down the rest of the hill. But if Naughty Tortie lifted her paw, the cake would hurtle into the traffic on the main road and make an awful mess.

'Of course,' he said. 'Come on, everyone, let's have some cake. You too, Naughty Tortie.'

Mr Pattacake carefully picked up the cake, while Naughty Tortie turned on her purriest, smoochiest charm as she followed the little crowd of children back to Jack's house.

Mr Pattacake set the table and put out the paper hats and blew up the balloons, which were Jack's favourite colours of blue and yellow, and just a few purple ones too. There were party poppers and paper plates with **Happy Birthday** written on them, as well as plastic cups for the drinks.

Then Mr Pattacake placed the cake onto the table and wedged something against the real wheels, while Jack's mum fetched a knife.

He left the **BIG IDEA** in the van.

Jack carefully cut his cake in half and then his mum cut it into small pieces, and handed them out on the paper plates.

She was looking worried again. 'I'm really no good at party games,' she said. 'I do wish we had the entertainer.'

Mr Pattacake just smiled and went out to his van.

The children played pass the parcel and musical chairs and pin the tail on the donkey.

When their cake had settled, Mr Pattacake said. 'I have a surprise. Come and see.'

Everyone followed him to the back door and ran outside.

On the lawn, stood a giant bouncy castle. It wobbled gently as Treacle sat on top, washing his paw.

Jack ran to it and stared. 'It's made of jelly!' he said, poking at it. 'A giant jelly bouncy castle!'

'I made it with extra strong jelly crystals,' said Mr Pattacake. 'So I'll be the first one to test it out.'

He took off his shoes and climbed onto the jelly, which wobbled even more and CATapulted Treacle into the air. He landed on his feet on the lawn, looking surprised whilst the children giggled.

Mr Pattacake wobbled. Then just as it seemed he would fall off, he began to bounce, leaping into the air, doing summersaults and handstands. He did pike jumps and front and back drops. His big chef's hat flew off when he did a half twist, and it spun through the air and landed in the pond. He was enjoying himself so much that he forgot about his bruises.

'And now,' said Mr Pattacake, stopping for a moment to get all the children's attention. 'I'm going to do a special trick called a *barani*. Please don't try this unless you are really good at trampolining.'

He began to bounce again, higher and higher. Then he bounced up, began a summersault and twisted in the air, landing again on his feet.

Everyone cheered.

Mr Pattacake bowed and climbed down off the jelly. He was out of breath and wiped his forehead with a hanky.

'Can I have a go, please?' asked Jack.

'Of course. You are the birthday boy, Jack,' said Mr Pattacake with a chuckle.

Jack carefully climbed onto the jelly and began jumping up and down.

'It's fantastic!' he said, beaming.

Soon everyone was having a go, and there were squeals and giggles as they all bounced up and down.

Mr Pattacake smiled with satisfaction. 'My pond liner made a good jelly mould.'

'Thank you, Mr Pattacake,' said Jack's mum. 'Not only did you make the food, but you sorted out the entertainment too!'

'And here's your hat, Mr Pattacake,' said Jack, who had fished it out of the pond. It was covered with green, slimy pond weed so Mr Pattacake took it carefully between two fingers and pulled a disgusted face. 'I don't think I'll wear it until it's been washed,' he said.

And as the children jumped and laughed, Treacle gently strummed his lute under the shade of an apple tree, while Naughty Tortie lay on her back in a patch of warm sunlight, cleaning her claws.

MR PATTACAKE

Stephanie Baudet

Sweet Cherry
Publishing

Published by Sweet Cherry Publishing Limited
Unit E, Vulcan Business Complex
Vulcan Road
Leicester, LE5 3EB
United Kingdom

First published in the UK in 2013
ISBN: 978-1-78226-057-8
©Stephanie Baudet 2014
Illustrations ©Creative Books
Illustrated by Ojoswi Sur & Joy Das

Mr Pattacake and the Dog's Dinner Disaster

Printed in India by Ajanta Offset and Packagings Limited

Pattacake, Pattacake, baker's man,
Bake me a cake as fast as you can;
Pat it and prick it and mark it with P,
Put it in the oven for you and for me.

Pattacake, Pattacake, baker's man,
Bake me a cake as fast as you can;
Roll it up, roll it up;
And throw it in a pan!

Pattacake, Pattacake, baker's man.

MR PATTACAKE
and the
DOG'S DINNER
DISASTER

'Ook, Eacle,' said Mr Pattacake, hopping from one foot to the other in excitement, his big chef's hat wobbling. What he was trying to say was, 'Look, Treacle,' but he had a mouthful of cornflakes, so that's why it came out all funny. As well as the muffled words, a little spattering of cornflakes came out of his mouth too.

He waved a letter in the air while doing the silly little dance he always did when he was excited.

Treacle, his ginger cat, had to jump out of the way of his big feet. He then yawned, showing that there were no cornflakes in *his* mouth. In fact, there was nothing at all in his mouth. It was about time Mr Pattacake gave him *his* breakfast.

Treacle knew that the letter must mean a cooking job for Mr Pattacake. He was excited too, but didn't show it in the same way that his owner did. He was a quiet sort of cat, but he *did* smile to himself. When Mr Pattacake did some cooking there was always something in it for him.

'A pet food company called 𝔸ℕ𝕚𝕄𝔼𝔸𝕃𝕊 wants me to invent some delicious new food for pets,' said Mr Pattacake, excitedly, having now swallowed his cornflakes. 'People are complaining that their pets are refusing eat because they are bored with the same food. That's definitely a job for us, Treacle, and you can be the chief cat food taster.'

Treacle licked his lips in delight. His tummy rumbled at the very thought. That was just the kind of job he liked.

Mr Pattacake straightened his yellow and black checked waistcoat and put on his big white apron. It was time to make his to-do list.

'First we have to invent some names for the food,' he said, picking up a pen and sitting down at

It didn't take him long. Mr Pattacake's imagination worked very fast.

'Listen, Treacle. What do you think? We can have,

Dog's Dinner,

Cat's Casserole,

Rabbit's Rations,

Bird's Breakfast,

Fish's Feast,

and Snake's Supper.'

Treacle sat on a chair washing his whiskers and paused to look up briefly as Mr Pattacake finished reading out the list.

'I knew you would like them,' said Mr Pattacake, smiling at Treacle. He understood cats very well – he even knew what they were thinking.

Mr Pattacake went off in his little yellow van to buy the ingredients. Then he got to work straight away.

15

Soon, Mr Pattacake had six big pans bubbling on the stove. He'd put in lots of delicious things that he knew each of the pets would love – plus a sprinkling of this and a dash of that. He'd also thrown in a handful of flavouring and just a shake of his magic ingredient.

Animals were fussy - he'd owned many of them in his time. Dogs, cats, mice, rabbits, a Shetland pony, and even a pot-bellied pig. So this job was just the thing for him. He was an **EXPERT** on animals.

The Cat's Casserole took the longest time to get right because the chief cat food taster was very particular. Treacle shrugged and shook his head, and swished his tail and even hissed as he tasted Mr Pattacake's different ideas.

It was a long time before he began to purr softly with approval, and by then he hardly had the energy left because he was too full.

Some of his friends came in too and gave their opinion. As the smells wafted out into the street they brought in one or two dogs as well – Bobby, the Jack Russell, from number ten, Mrs Hall's springer spaniel, Tia, and even a few that Mr Pattacake had never seen before. A white rabbit called Snowy hopped in, and an escaped green budgie too. Soon Mr Pattacake's kitchen looked like a zoo.

'Shoo!' said Mr Pattacake, flapping his hands, and looking round to make sure there were no snakes slithering around on the floor. 'I'm trying to work here.' But the animals would not move until he had given each of them a little taste.

They chewed. They rolled their eyes. They swallowed. Then they all jumped up and down with excitement - each one gave their approval. They all thought the food was **DELICIOUS!**

Meanwhile, Mr Pattacake got out six giant plastic pots with lids, and wrote on some labels, *dog, cat, rabbit, bird, fish, snake,* which he then stuck on the lids.

Finally, Treacle politely asked the animals to leave and showed them out of the door. He and Mr Pattacake had lots to do.

But the green budgie stayed behind, eyeing Treacle from the top of the cupboard. He didn't like being told what to do, especially by a cat.

The green budgie then flew down on to the worktop. Treacle tried to ignore him, and Mr Pattacake was busy, so neither of them noticed him meddling with the pot lids.

At last he flew out of the window.

'Right,' said Mr Pattacake, picking up one of the big saucepans. 'Where is the first pot for the Dog's Dinner? All the lids are in order so you can put them on, Treacle.'

Treacle pushed a pot forward and Mr Pattacake tipped the food into it. At last, when all the pots were full, Treacle put on the lids and jumped on them to fasten them tightly.

Except…

Treacle was a cat and he couldn't read. Oh dear!
What a muddle!

Mr Pattacake, unaware of the mix-up,
loaded the pots into his little van and drove off to
ANiMEALS.

Job done!

Treacle curled up in a patch of warm sunlight. He had eaten sooooo much. There was something worrying him however, but he just sighed and closed his eyes. Nothing ever worried him for long.

Mr Pattacake wasn't worrying about anything. He was thinking about the money he would make from the recipes when ANiMEALS saw how successful the food was. Pet owners would be queuing up to buy the food and he would be even more well-known than he was now.

But he waited…

And waited…

But there was no news from ANiMEALS.
What had gone wrong?

Then one day Mr Pattacake received a phone
call.

'Are you Mr Pattacake? The one who made the Dog's Dinner?' asked the lady on the phone.

Ah! A satisfied customer at last, Mr Pattacake thought to himself. 'Yes, I am,' he said happily

'You'd better come and have a look at my dog, Benny,' she said.

She didn't sound pleased at all. Whatever could be wrong?

Mr Pattacake and Treacle went round to the lady's house. Treacle normally didn't like dogs very much, but he was curious to know what was wrong, and his nagging little worry had returned.

When the lady opened the front door, Mr Pattacake looked round, expecting the dog to come running to see who it was, as dogs do.

'Oh, he's not in the house,' said the lady, shaking her head. 'It's very strange. Come and take a look.' She led them out to the back garden.

In one corner was a big fish pond.

Benny, the Labrador, was in the water. At least, Mr Pattacake assumed it was Benny. In some places where there should have been golden fur, there were pale pink scales instead. Benny was swimming around the pond, opening and closing his mouth without making a sound, and on his head sat a green frog.

'Benny!' Mr Pattacake patted his knee, trying to get him to come out of the water.

Benny's doggy side tried to wag his tail, but it was difficult to do so in the pond, so it just resulted in spraying water all over Mr Pattacake and the lady.

They both looked surprised and tried to brush the water off their clothes.

Treacle, on the other hand, being a clever cat who hated getting wet, had seen it coming and got out of the way just in time.

'He won't come out,' said the lady, frowning. She backed away from the pond a little too late. 'He loved your pet food, but I think there must have been some terrible mistake. He stays in the pond all the time now. He doesn't even want to go for walks anymore, and he's looking more and more like a fish every day.' She sounded very worried.

Mr Pattacake took off his big chef's hat and shook the water off it. Then he glared at Treacle, and Treacle felt that nagging little worry grow even bigger.

It couldn't be his fault though, could it? He was a cat, and cats couldn't read.

He hadn't been able to read the labels on the food pots, and Mr Pattacake rather foolishly hadn't checked.

'What are we going to do, Mr Pattacake?' said the lady. 'I want my lovely Benny back, not this dog fish. My nice *furry* Benny, who likes going for walks.'

'Don't worry, I'll put it right,' said Mr Pattacake, trying to sound convincing, although he wasn't exactly sure what he was going to do. He needed to get his imagination to work on it.

But before he had time to think, he received a text message.

It read:

**MR PATTACAKE. WHAT DID YOU PUT
IN THE CAT'S CASSEROLE? MY CAT, FLUFFY,
KEEPS TRYING TO FLY. PLEASE COME
AND HELP.**

Mr Pattacake gasped with horror. He was no longer his usual happy self. His big chef's hat didn't wobble with excitement anymore, but rather trembled with worry. What had gone wrong with the pets' meals?

He and Treacle got in the little yellow van and drove to the boy's house. When they arrived, a small crowd had gathered on the pavement and were all looking up, their mouths open in fear. On the edge of the roof stood a black cat, its front paws held up like wings.

'Come down, Fluffy!' the boy pleaded, his arms stretched out towards the strange creature on the roof. 'You can't fly. You're a cat.'

Fluffy was not so fluffy anymore. It was difficult to see at that height, but Mr Pattacake thought his fur looked more like feathers, and his front legs had widened to look more like wings, but not enough to make him to fly though.

Fluffy answered the boy, but instead of a meow, it was a tweet.

Now everyone knows that cats can jump from high places and always land on their feet, but this was definitely *too* high.

Just then, Mr Pattacake had one of his sudden ideas.

'I know what to do!' he shouted, trying to save the situation. 'Go and fetch a large bed sheet,' he told the boy. 'The biggest you can find!'

The boy looked doubtful, but then nodded and ran inside his house. He soon returned with an enormous white cotton sheet.

'Now,' instructed Mr Pattacake, opening the sheet out, 'everyone must take an edge of the sheet and we'll all hold it like a safety net so we can catch Fluffy.'

Everyone grabbed part of the sheet and held it out taut just in time before Fluffy spread her wing-like paws and took off from the roof.

She didn't fly of course. Despite flapping her paws rapidly, she just dropped straight down onto the sheet like a lead weight. She was so frightened that she just bounced right out again, but this time she landed perfectly on her feet on the pavement and scooted away in a flash.

'Thank you, Mr Pattacake,' said the boy, looking relieved. 'But you'll have to do something before she tries to fly again. She will hurt herself. I want a fluffy cat, not a bird.'

'Don't worry, I'll put it right,' said Mr Pattacake, trying to sound reassuring, and he and Treacle went home so they could start thinking.

Before Mr Pattacake could begin, however, he received an email. It was from a small girl called Katy.

'Mr Pattacake. My rabbit, Bounce, loved the Rabbit Rations that you invented, but now he's not acting like a rabbit anymore.'

Once again, Mr Pattacake and Treacle set off in the little yellow van to the pet owner's house. Mr Pattacake could see that something very wrong had happened, and that this wouldn't be the end of it.

When the little girl opened the door, a rabbit came running to greet them, barking like a dog. He didn't hop like a rabbit, he *ran*. His once long ears were shorter, and his bobbly tail was trying to wag.

'He loved your food, Mr Pattacake,' said Katy, bending down to stroke Treacle, who purred loudly. 'But he's acting more like a dog than a rabbit. I like dogs, but I preferred my rabbit. He's more like a doggit now.'

Treacle didn't like dogs but he didn't mind rabbits. So now he was confused, not knowing whether to spit or not.

'Don't worry, I'll put it right,' said Mr Pattacake, trying to comfort her. He then went home to think about what to do. It was getting very worrying.

'Somehow the pots got mixed up,' he said to Treacle, who hung his head in shame. But it wasn't his fault. After all, cat's couldn't read.

Just then, the doorbell rang.

'I'm Mr Martin,' said the man on the doorstep. 'I gave my goldfish your new Fish's Feast, and now he… well, you'd better come and see for yourself.'

Mr Pattacake and Treacle followed Mr Martin to his house, anticipating the worst once again. Mr Pattacake gasped when he saw a shattered fish bowl on the floor, and a puddle of water surrounding it.

'This is Goldy,' said Mr Martin, pointing at the creature on the soaked carpet. 'But something has happened to him since he ate your fish food.'

Something had happened to him indeed.

He was still gold, at least, but now he had completely outgrown his bowl and seemed to be able to breathe air. What's more, he had grown little legs and was hopping about all over the floor, his little nose twitching. He was still mostly covered in scales, but he had grown a fluffy tail, and long furry ears were sprouting out of his head.

'Oh dear,' said Mr Pattacake in disbelief. 'What a curious creature.'

'Yes,' said Mr Martin. 'But I want my goldfish back. You have to do something about it, Mr Pattacake. He keeps digging holes in the garden.'

'Don't worry, I'll put it right,' said Mr Pattacake. But now he was getting more and more worried. *How* was he going to put it right?

By now he knew that he could expect a couple more complaints, and sure enough, a letter arrived the next day. Usually, a letter caused great excitement, as it often meant a new job for him and Treacle. But this time he opened it with dread, not wanting to find out what was inside.

'Dear Mr Pattacake,' he read, cautiously:

'You have to do something. Ever since I gave some of your Snake's Supper to my snake, he's been acting really strangely.'

When they arrived at the man's house, Treacle backed away into a corner as soon as he saw the snake. He had never seen a snake before, but he was sure that they shouldn't look like this one did.

Mr Pattacake had never been up close to a snake before either, but one thing he knew for sure, was that they didn't have legs. No snake had legs. If they did, they were a lizard, not a snake. Snakes wriggled and slithered. This one walked. It walked with its tail in the air. A fluffy tail. Also, Mr Pattacake knew that snakes hissed. That was the only sound they made. They certainly did *not* meow.

'My goodness!' said Mr Pattacake in shock.

'You may well say that,' agreed the man. 'I have studied snakes all my life. I'm a herpetologist, and I have never seen anything like this before. How did you do it, Mr Pattacake?'

'Well, I ... I think things got a little bit mixed up in the kitchen,' he said, sheepishly, glaring at Treacle, who retreated further into the corner shamefacedly.

'You mean cat food was accidentally put into the pots for snake food? How interesting. I'd like to know what was in the food, Mr Pattacake. This is amazing. It's a scientific breakthrough!'

Mr Pattacake smiled for the first time in ages. At last, a pet owner who was not angry about the changes in their pet, but was actually *interested* in them.

'I'll give you the recipe,' he said, feeling more cheerful.

'But…' said the man. 'I do want my snake back though.'

'Don't worry, I'll put it right,' said Mr Pattacake, nodding as he and Treacle left.

There was really no point in setting his imagination to work until the last pet owner contacted him, so he waited.

The next day, the doorbell rang again.

On the step stood a small boy holding a birdcage. He blinked up at Mr Pattacake from under his mop of unruly brown hair.

'Look what your food has done to Tweety,' he said, holding up the heavy cage with great difficulty.

'Come in,' said Mr Pattacake, before even looking into the cage. 'I've been expecting you.'

He helped the boy lift the birdcage onto the worktop in the kitchen.

Inside was what could only be described as a *snudgie*. It had once been a blue budgie but most of its feathers had turned into scales, and its feet had completely disappeared. It opened its mouth and a long forked tongue flicked out.

Of course, it could no longer sit on its perch, but instead wriggled along the bottom of the cage. When it tried to tweet, only a soft hissing sound came out.

Treacle didn't like the creature at all. It didn't look anything like that naughty budgie which had refused to leave the kitchen when Mr Pattacake was making the food. That one had been green.

Then something stirred in the back of his mind. What had that green budgie been up to? The look on its face had reminded him of that sneaky tortoiseshell cat, Naughty Tortie, who he hadn't seen for a while.

'I want my budgie back, Mr Pattacake,' pleaded the boy. 'My mum doesn't like snakes.'

'Don't worry, I'll put it right,' said Mr Pattacake with a smile. Now was the time. All the pet owners had finally contacted him so he had to use his imagination to put the pets back as they were. It would need some extra strong ingredients.

Not only had the pet owners complained to Mr Pattacake, but they had all gone round to ANiMEALS to complain there too. The manager was almost exploding with rage.

'I've had hundreds of pet owners queuing up outside to make a complaint,' he said, waving his hand to indicate how long the queue had been. 'And they turned up with a very strange variety of animals. Who is responsible for this mistake?'

Mr Pattacake looked at Treacle, who thought that it wasn't very fair that he was being blamed. Everyone knew that cats couldn't read. And anyway, he had the feeling that someone else was responsible. He stared back at Mr Pattacake.

'Ah,' said Mr Pattacake. 'I may be partly to blame for not checking the labels, but I do believe that there has been some mischief going on here.'

He too was remembering the budgie who had refused to leave. He now remembered seeing, out of the corner of his eye, the budgie with a pot lid in his beak. He'd been too busy to think anything of it at the time.

'It doesn't matter whose fault it was now. All I know is that you must put it right, Mr Pattacake,' said the manager of ANiMEALS, sternly. 'The food was a great success, but we must make sure that the right pets get the right food this time.'

'So it was that mischievous budgie all along,' said Mr Pattacake when the manager had left. 'He swapped the lids and then I didn't check. So,

The Dog's Dinner went into the pot for rabbits.

The Cat's Casserole went into the snake food.

The Rabbit's Rations went into the fish food.

The Bird's Breakfast went into the cat's pot.

The Fish's Feast went into the dog's food.

And the Snake's Supper went into the bird's food.

Oh dear!'

Mr Pattacake thought and thought. How was he going to put this right? He really had to stretch his imagination. His big chef's hat wobbled as his brain whirred inside his head. Never had it had to work so hard before.

He thought…

And thought…

And thought…

And then he had a brilliant idea.

'Yippee!' He did his silly dance to show his excitement.

Soon, he and Treacle had the six pans out again.

This time, however, Mr Pattacake made sure that *he* checked the labels, and no little budgie, or anyone else for that matter, was allowed in his kitchen while he worked.

Just to make sure the recipes would work, he added some extra ingredients.

In the Dog's Dinner, he added a little piece of *bark*.

In the Cat's Casserole, he added a spoonful of *Mews-li*.

In the Rabbit's Rations, he added a handful of *hops*.

In the Bird's Breakfast, he added a dead *fly*.

He weighed the Fish's Feast very carefully on the *scales*.

And cooked the Snake's Supper until it *hissed*.

Then they took the whole lot back to **ANiMEALS** where the manager invited all the pet owners back, as well as their pets, to feed them the correct food.

The queue went right round the block and it took the whole day to feed each animal with the correct food, a process very carefully supervised by Mr Pattacake.

Then all they could do was to wait patiently.

Gradually things began to happen.

Benny, the dog, shook off his scales and barked excitedly at his owner, who looked relieved to have a normal dog again. But Benny absolutely *refused* to get in the bath to wash off the slimy pond weed!

Fluffy, the cat, became fluffy again, and stopped trying to fly.

Bounce, the rabbit, hopped about, twitching his little nose with familiar vigour.

Goldy, the goldfish, had a new bowl, and as he became smaller and scalier, his owner popped him back into the water, just before his fluffy tail disappeared.

The herpetologist reminded Mr Pattacake about the promised recipe, and then he happily wound his furless snake around his neck and went home.

cage once its legs had grown back so it could sit on its perch. The budgie began to preen its newly restored feathers.

Mr Pattacake and Treacle looked very closely at Tweety but could see no resemblance to that naughty *green* budgie who had mixed up the lids. The budgie that had reminded them of the troublesome cat, Naughty Tortie.

They knew they would have to watch out for that mischievous cat in future, whatever animal her spirit chose to inhabit.

MR PATTACAKE

Stephanie Baudet

Sweet Cherry
Publishing

Published by Sweet Cherry Publishing Limited
Unit E, Vulcan Business Complex
Vulcan Road
Leicester, LE5 3EB
United Kingdom

First published in the UK in 2013
ISBN: 978-1-78226-058-5
©Stephanie Baudet 2014
Illustrations ©Creative Books
Illustrated by Ojoswi Sur & Joy Das

Mr Pattacake and the Pirates

Printed in India by Ajanta Offset and Packagings Limited

Pattacake, Pattacake, baker's man,
Bake me a cake as fast as you can;
Pat it and prick it and mark it with P,
Put it in the oven for you and for me.

Pattacake, Pattacake, baker's man,
Bake me a cake as fast as you can;
Roll it up, roll it up;
And throw it in a pan!

Pattacake, Pattacake, baker's man.

MR PATTACAKE
and the
PIRATES

Mr Pattacake and his ginger cat, Treacle, stood looking up at the enormous cruise ship in the harbour. It was all white, and towered above them like a great floating city.

Mr Pattacake had a big grin on his face, and his big chef's hat wobbled with excitement. He would have done the silly dance he always did when he was excited, but he forced himself to stand still, in case anyone was watching from any one of the hundreds of windows on the side of the ship.

'What do you think, Treacle?' he said. 'I can't believe I've been asked to be the ship's chef! Aren't we lucky?'

Treacle was not certain whether he thought they had been lucky or not. Like most cats, he didn't like water, and the idea of floating on it made him feel a little seasick already. However, the thought of all those tasty morsels that Mr Pattacake would be sure to give him whilst cooking, had persuaded him to come along. Besides, it was such a big ship that perhaps he would forget he was on the water.

Mr Pattacake reached into his pocket for the letter he had received from the ship's captain. His previous chef had stayed behind on a tropical island so he desperately needed a replacement

Letter in hand, Mr Pattacake bent to lift up his old, brown suitcase, as well as the small bag Treacle had brought (holding his bed and his food bowl). He marched jauntily to the gangplank, where a sailor in a smart white uniform stood on guard.

'I'm the new chef,' said Mr Pattacake, 'and this is my assistant, Treacle.'

Treacle puffed out his chest with pride. He'd never been called *that* before.

The sailor looked at them both and then at the letter, shaking his head all the while. He seemed to be trying not to smile.

'Not this ship, sir,' he said. 'This is The Royal
Queen. Your letter says *The Sea Snake*. That ship over
there, sir.'

Mr Pattacake looked where the sailor was
pointing.

A small, rusty tub of a ship huddled behind the
grand cruise liner. It flew no flag, and had a slight list
to one side.

'Oh,' said Mr Pattacake, disappointed. He hoped it might be more comfortable than it looked.

When he and Treacle reached the gangplank of *The Sea Snake*, it looked a little rickety, with a lean to one side like the ship, and part of the handrail missing. Unlike *The Royal Queen* it had no sailor on guard, so Mr Pattacake and Treacle staggered up to the deck, grasping what there was of the handrail with a free hand.

Mr Pattacake, that is. Treacle had to use all four paws for walking, but luckily cats have better balance than humans.

The deck was deserted and there was silence except for the creak of the wooden hull and snapping of the rigging.

'Hello…?' called Mr Pattacake, a little anxiously.

A head appeared through a hatch.

'Oh hello,' said Mr Pattacake. 'My name is Mr Pattacake and I'm the new chef.'

The sailor climbed out onto the deck. He was not wearing a smart white uniform, or a uniform of any kind, for that matter. He wore torn cropped pants, a rather grubby, stripy shirt and a red bandana around his head. Both the sailor and his clothes looked in need of a good wash.

'And you be welcome!' said the sailor, smiling.

'I be Mucky Mick. I'll show you to your cabin.'

Mr Pattacake relaxed. Maybe this wasn't going to be such a bad job after all, if one friendly sailor was anything to go by.

The cabin was small, but it did have a porthole – a round grubby one, right at water level. It would not be wise to open it, and was rusted shut anyway, but provided a little light in the gloomy room.

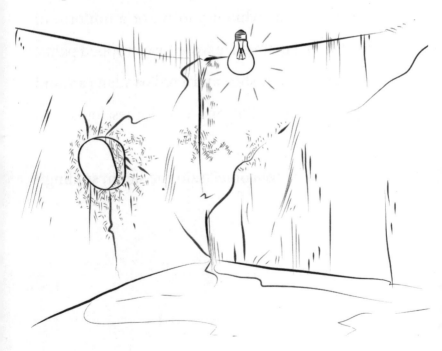

Mr Pattacake flung his suitcase onto the small, narrow bed, opened the lid, and began unpacking. Then he took Treacle's bed and bowl out of the bag and placed them in a corner on the floor.

'I expect the crew will want a nice dinner,' he said, 'and I've made my usual list.' Mr Pattacake always made lists, and this time he had planned the meals for a whole week and sent a list of required ingredients to the captain in advance.

'So, it should be all plain sailing,' said Mr Pattacake, smiling at his own wit as he put on his big white chef's apron. Treacle rolled his eyes and pawed at his food bowl.

'You're hungry,' said Mr Pattacake, nodding at him. He always knew what Treacle was saying, although sometimes it was clear to everyone.

'Welcome!' came a deep voice from the doorway. Mr Pattacake spun round. Standing with his hands on his hips was a very big man dressed almost the same as the first sailor, except that he wore a wide black leather belt around his huge belly.

'I be Captain Sam Stinky,' said the man, thrusting out is hand.

Mr Pattacake reached out and shook it, but then wished he hadn't. The captain's grip was very sweaty and so strong it almost crushed his fingers.

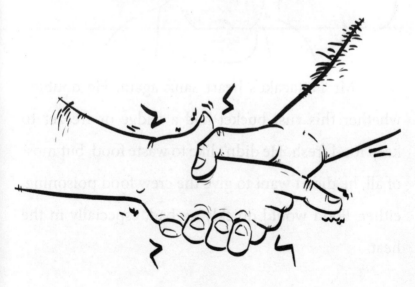

'I hope you received my letter about the provisions?' said Mr Pattacake.

'Y'Arr,' said the captain. 'All that fancy stuff! We got some of it, but you'll have to make do. We've still got food left over from the last trip to use up.'

Mr Pattacake's heart sank again. He doubted whether this rust bucket had a fridge or freezer to keep food fresh. He didn't like to waste food, but most of all, he didn't want to give the crew food poisoning, either. Food would quickly go bad, especially in the heat.

'What you got planned for dinner tonight, Mr P?' asked the captain.

'My name is Mr Pattacake,' said Mr Pattacake. 'I prefer to be called by my full name. And for dinner… it's supposed to be lamb casserole… if you have any lamb.'

The captain just grinned and left, and soon they felt a judder as the ship's engines started up and they pulled away from the dock. Mr Pattacake, followed by Treacle, went to find the galley so he could get to work on the dinner.

As they passed an open hatch, they saw two sailors hoisting a flag up the ship's mast. It flapped and cracked in the sharp breeze.

Mr Pattacake skidded to a stop when he noticed that it was black, and had a white skull and crossbones on it. His big chef's hat wobbled dangerously. He knew instantly what that meant. This was a pirate ship! The skull, he noticed, was unusual in that it looked friendly. It had a slight twinkle in its eye sockets.

'We have to get off! Stop the ship!' he cried, clambering up the stairs and running onto the deck.

'What's up?' It was another sailor whom they hadn't met.

'Is that the Jolly Roger flying up there?'

The sailor nodded. 'That be it,' he said with a grin that showed his rotten teeth.

'Then this is a pirate ship… and you are pirates,' said Mr Pattacake.

'Y'Arr, but we be good pirates,' said the sailor. 'We don't do no plunderin'. We be off to the treasure-hunting competition on Hawiti Island in the South Pacific.'

Mr Pattacake paused and relaxed a little. A Pacific island sounded nice, and if they were good pirates, well… perhaps it would be all right.

The pirate sniggered and thumped him on the back, nearly knocking him over. 'Besides,' he said, 'we can't stop the ship now. It's too late.'

It was true. Mr Pattacake could only just make out the docks in the distance. He went back downstairs... or below deck and soon found the galley. There was no fear of getting lost on this ship. It was so small.

Like the rest of the ship, the galley was rusty, but on top of the rust was a thick layer of something else. When Mr Pattacake scratched at it with his finger nail, he realised that it was where food had spilt and splashed all over the place and had never been cleaned up. He wrinkled up his nose in disgust. He was going to need a chisel to get this clean!

As well as that, the galley was crammed with boxes and rubbish, as if it was used as a store room as well as a cooking room. Treacle started sniffing round. Where there was rotten food there were mice!

Mr Pattacake rolled up his sleeves and started cleaning, using an old knife to scrape off the thick layer of spilt food. It was revolting!

Then he looked in the cupboards. There wasn't much there. His list of foods had been ignored. He sighed with disappointment. There was lamb, but it had been salted to stop it going bad. He would have to use all his chef's expertise to make a tasty meal out of this lot!

Eventually, after soaking it well to get the salt out, he made a lamb casserole. He also found some apples and grapes and two rather dried up oranges, so he made a fruit salad for dessert. How could the captain have ignored his list of food?

The first meal, however, was a roaring success, with the whole crew giving him three cheers in the usual noisy pirate fashion. They snatched the bandanas off their heads and waved them about. With the third riotous cheer, many of them threw plates into the air, which smashed as they landed on the deck. The captain was as noisy and wild as any of them, smiling round at his happy men.

Mr Pattacake gave a small bow, careful not to dislodge his chef's hat. They did seem like good pirates and, in fact, they were the first pirates he had ever met. Pirates usually had a bad name but it just showed that you shouldn't believe all you hear.

Mr Pattacake and Treacle settled down to their routine as the ship made its way to the South Pacific.

The weather got warmer as they got further south and Mr Pattacake sweated under his big floppy hat. Eventually, he took it off altogether, along with his yellow and black checked waistcoat. It was forty degrees on the deck and much hotter in the galley. 'Ah, that's better,' he said, feeling much fresher.

Treacle couldn't take off his fur coat so he spent most of the day asleep in a shady corner, just rousing himself to eat now and again.

Finally, they arrived at Hawiti Island. The captain turned off the engine and they sailed into the bay, to drop anchor alongside several other ships.

Mr Pattacake went out on deck and looked around. These were all pirate ships bringing pirates to take part in the treasure-hunting competition. They didn't all look as friendly as the pirates on his ship.

'Are you going ashore, Mr Pattacake?' asked Captain Sam Stinky, joining him at the ship's rail.

It did look inviting, with the pale yellow sandy beach and palm trees, some of them heavy with coconuts. The water was so clear that you could see the seabed, even though it was quite deep where they were anchored. Brilliantly-coloured tropical fish swam about in the warm turquoise water. The cloudless sky was a deep blue. Mr Pattacake had seen pictures of places like this, but he had never seen them for himself. He sighed with satisfaction. This was certainly a great job. Any worries he'd had about it had completely gone.

He watched the pirates pouring off the ships and clambering into small boats that took them ashore. Then they ran barefoot up the beach, their sabres swinging at their sides and their lank, oily hair tied back with bandanas. They exchanged cunning and evil glances as they shouted wildly to each other. Mr Pattacake couldn't hear what they were saying, but he could tell by the tone that there was some serious rivalry in this competition. This was no friendly game.

'No,' said Mr Pattacake to the captain. 'I'll stay on board. I can prepare a victory dinner for the crew.'

Captain Stinky nodded. 'We be the winners many a time,' he said. 'My men are good at followin' maps.' He pulled a big map out of his pocket and spread it out so that Mr Pattacake could see.

There was the outline of the island with trees and hills marked on it, and even a small river. Right in the centre of the map was a big X. Captain Stinky jabbed at it with his finger. 'Here be the treasure,' he said.

'Who put the treasure there?' asked Mr Pattacake.

'Y'Arr,' said the captain. 'That be the president of the Piratical Society. He gets together some treasure...'

The captain hesitated. 'From others' plunderin' and buries it somewhere different each year. The first pirate to find it claims it for his crew.'

Shortly afterwards, someone blew a whistle and they were off. With their spades in their hands, they headed for the centre of the island, a member of each crew clutching a copy of the map.

Mr Pattacake went below deck to the galley and began to think about the victory dinner. There was one thing which puzzled him about the treasure hunt. Would all these nasty pirates accept the winner? It seemed to him that a bunch of rascals like this would not be so fair-minded, but would want to get their hands on the treasure at any cost.

In the galley was a fresh fish which one of the pirates had caught earlier that day. It was a red emperor, and big enough to feed the whole crew, so Mr Pattacake gutted it and gently cooked it.

Then he placed it on a bed of rice on a huge silver platter, along with some dried peas which he had soaked and made into mushy peas.

In the quiet of the afternoon, he did venture ashore to pick up a coconut he'd spotted lying in the sand. He climbed down the rope ladder and then swam ashore. It wasn't far, and such a pleasure to cool down in the water, but the return journey carrying the coconut, had been very tricky indeed.

With the coconut milk he made a sauce for the fish dish and then he decorated the platter with coconut shavings.

There was tinned pineapple for dessert.

What a feast! Mr Pattacake looked at it proudly. He'd been very clever to make such a meal out of practically nothing.

Treacle was also very satisfied. He had eaten a few bits of fish that Mr Pattacake had cut off, as well as catching a mouse scurrying around under a cupboard.

They were both admiring the food display when they heard shouts and the stamping of feet as the pirates swarmed up the rope ladder and onto the deck.

The first pirate to appear was Mucky Mick, so Mr Pattacake asked whether they had won. He was anxious to present the victory dinner.

Mucky Mick shook his head miserably. 'We could have won,' he said. 'We were on the right track. We could have got there first, if they played fair.'

'Have you ever won?' asked Mr Pattacake.

'Well,' said the pirate, 'not exactly.'

Mmm, thought Mr Pattacake. That's not what the captain said earlier. They may be good pirates but they were not exactly honest.

He tried to cheer them up with his non-victory dinner.

'We be the winners next year,' said Captain Sam Stinky, smiling broadly.

They had almost finished the first course, when there was more shouting and the thunder of feet on the deck.

'Who forgot to pull up the rope ladder?' growled the captain, just as a bunch of fearsome pirates burst into the room, waving their cutlasses menacingly.

They stopped in front of Mr Pattacake, whose big chef's hat trembled with fear.

'We heard about you,' said one of the pirates. 'Best chef on the high seas, so we've come to get you. You be wasted on this bunch of no-good sea dogs.'

Before Mr Pattacake knew what was happening, he was seized by the arms and swept out of the room and onto the deck.

They forced him down the rope ladder and into a small boat bobbing on the water below.

Despite being frightened out of his wits, Mr Pattacake thought about Treacle, but decided that the cat was better off staying with the good pirates. Besides, a cat couldn't climb down a rope ladder. He had never seen it done before at anyway.

The pirates rowed towards another ship anchored nearby called *The Skull Duggery*, where Mr Pattacake was forced to climb *up* a rope ladder.

On the deck he was greeted by the fiercest looking man he had ever seen. One dark eye glared out from under a bushy black eyebrow, the other being covered by an eye patch. His cold smile showed a mouth full of rotten teeth, with some missing altogether, and a big bushy beard covered the lower half of his face.

On his shoulder sat a green and red parrot, also eyeing Mr Pattacake fiercely. Something in the parrot's face reminded him of someone, although he couldn't think who it was at that moment.

The captain spoke first. 'I be Captain Crook.'

'And I'm Polly Wally,' interrupted the parrot rudely.

'Shuddup!' roared the captain, and Polly Wally hid behind his head, muttering to himself.

'You be our cook now,' said the captain. 'And you'd better make sure you cook well, otherwise it's the plank for you!'

Mr Pattacake had heard enough about pirates to know what that was. If you didn't please them, they made you walk along a plank jutting out from the side of the ship, until you fell headlong into the sea!

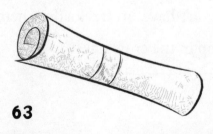

'I'll do my best, Captain,' said Mr Pattacake, trying to speak without his voice shaking.

Suddenly, something was thrown at his feet. It was poor Treacle.

'This your cat?' asked a pirate. 'Found him following you.'

Captain Crook glared down at Treacle. 'If he comes aboard, he works,' he said cold-heartedly. 'We don't have no freeloaders here. He can take his turn up in the crow's nest.'

Mr Pattacake looked up the tall mast to the small platform at the very top. The crow's nest. That was where the lookout stood scanning the horizon for land or other ships. What good would Treacle be up there? Everyone knew that cats couldn't talk.

Polly Wally was curious about Treacle and had climbed down from the captain's shoulder and was waddling towards him. From a safe distance, it suddenly darted forward and plucked at the fur of Treacle's tail, making the cat leap around.

All the pirates laughed for rather too long. Mr Pattacake didn't think it was that funny. Treacle didn't think so either, but he put up with the indignity for now. He thought there was something familiar about the bird too.

If Mr Pattacake thought the galley on *The Sea Snake* was bad, this one was far worse. He wrinkled up his nose, put on his rubber gloves, and set to work cleaning up as much as he could.

At least there was more food in the cupboards on this ship, so Mr Pattacake decided to make a shepherd's pie. It came out of the oven golden brown, and he took it out to the hungry pirates and proudly placed it on the table.

The loud chatter stopped abruptly.

'What be that?' asked the captain gruffly.

'It's shepherd's pie, Captain,' said Mr Pattacake, beginning to feel that something was wrong.

'Shepherd's pie?' roared Captain Crook. 'We be no shepherds, herdin' up sheep! We be pirates!' He thumped his chest and all the others did the same.

Nevertheless, they tucked into the shepherd's pie and scraped the dish so well that it hardly needed washing.

'Tomorrow you make us something fit for pirates, otherwise you walk the plank,' said the captain, wiping remnants of mashed potato off his beard with the back of his hand.

Mr Pattacake didn't know any pirate recipes so the next day he made the next best thing – fisherman's pie, followed by Swiss roll and custard.

'Fishermen?' yelled the captain. 'We be no fishermen, except when we need to eat.' Again he and all the pirates gobbled up the food as if they enjoyed it. When Mr Pattacake brought out the Swiss roll and custard, he said, 'Here's a nice Pirate's roll I baked.'

The captain smirked. 'You're learnin', he chortled.

The next day it was Treacle's turn as lookout up the crow's nest. He tried to tell the pirates that he wouldn't be able to shout, 'Land ahoy!' because he was a cat, and couldn't talk, but nobody could understand his loud, desperate meows. They just pushed him up the rigging and watched until he reached the crow's nest. He was relieved that there were no actual crows, but there *was* Polly Wally, who had flown up to perch on the rail, screeching at him.

Treacle suddenly remembered who Polly Wally reminded him of. It was that mischievous tortoiseshell cat, Naughty Tortie, who was always poking her nose in and causing trouble!

He sat trying to ignore the parrot, which kept edging forward to dart little pecks at Treacle's fur with its huge curved beak.

Later, Mr Pattacake was just serving a ploughman's lunch, which he had cleverly renamed Plunderer's Lunch, when a great juddering shook the whole ship, sending the meal onto the floor. Splat! (That was the pickle!)

'Hard to port!' yelled a pirate.

'Who be on lookout duty, Evil Ed?' yelled the captain. 'Lettin' us nearly run aground.'

'It be that useless cat, Captain,' said Evil Ed.

'Right! Can't have no slackers on this ship! Make ready the plank!'

'Oh no! Please Captain,' pleaded Mr Pattacake. 'He's only a cat and can't talk. He doesn't like water either.'

'No excuses!' The captain glowered at him. 'None of us like being in the water. That be the idea of the punishment.'

Poor Treacle was dragged down from the crow's nest, his eyes wide with fear. Then Evil Ed put a blindfold on him so he couldn't see when he reached the end of the plank.

He was put on the plank and given a little nudge. The whole crew gathered round. They'd seen plenty of people walk the plank, but never a cat. Then they began to chant, 'Walk the plank, walk the plank,' as Treacle crept forward towards the edge of it – and the sea.

Then Mr Pattacake had one of his bright ideas. While all the pirates were watching Treacle, he dashed up to the wheel deck. As he thought, no one was steering the ship. He grabbed the wheel and began to turn it towards the shore, pulling hard on the handles that stuck out all the way around.

He could see Treacle nearing the end of the plank, warily putting out one paw after another, not knowing when he would topple into the sea.

The sailors were so absorbed in watching Treacle and urging him on that they didn't notice that the ship was getting very near to shore on the opposite side.

SPLASH, Treacle fell into the sea to a great cheer from the pirates, who crowded to the ship's rail to see what had happened to him.

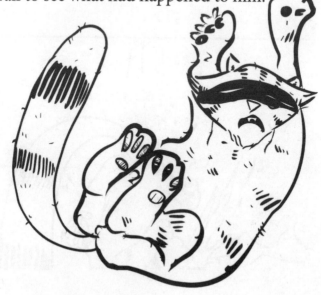

Captain Crook was leaning right over the rail just as, with a big judder, the ship ran aground on a small island. As more of his body was over the rail than on the ship, he toppled over into the water. He made a much bigger splash than Treacle had, and a lot more noise

Although cats don't like water, they *can* swim. But Captain Crook couldn't. Mr Pattacake could hear his cries for help as he himself scrambled down the rope ladder. He was getting very good at climbing up and down those by now.

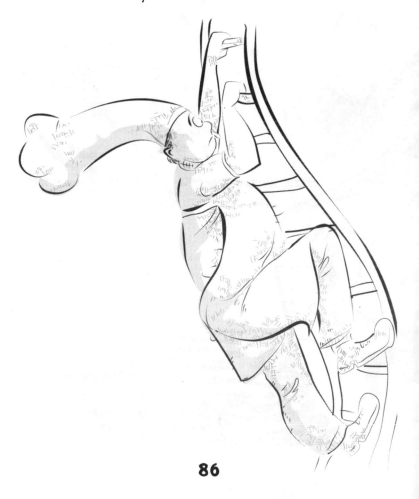

He jumped into the shallow water and waded ashore to join Treacle, who was already there, standing on the small beach drying his fur with his tongue. As Mr Pattacake sat down beside him, panting, Treacle paused briefly, looked up at him, and smiled his cat's smile.

They watched as the captain was hauled aboard by his crew, who had thrown him a rope. Then they all swarmed over to the side of the ship facing the island and stared at Mr Pattacake and Treacle, sitting on the beach. They were all afraid of getting into the water and coming after them.

'They're not so fierce now, Treacle,' said Mr Pattacake, laughing.

Captain Crook was waving his fist and shouting something neither of them could hear, which was probably just as well, and Polly Wally, who had flown off when he had fallen into the sea, was once again perched on its master's shoulder, making as much noise as anyone.

Later that evening, when the tide rose, *The Skull Duggery* and her band of pirates floated off and sailed away.

'We're on our own now, Treacle,' said Mr Pattacake. 'Let's hope someone rescues us before long.'

They ate the flesh and drank the milk of the coconuts for two days. Even Treacle realised that it was that, or starve to death. Mr Pattacake decided that tropical islands in the South Pacific were nice for a while but not to live on permanently. On your own without any food or water, they could be very harsh places.

For several days, the two sat on the beach and looked out to sea, hoping to see the shape of a ship coming over the horizon. They were fed up with coconuts, and afraid to eat any of the berries growing there in case they were poisonous.

Then one day a ship came into view. As it got closer, Mr Pattacake climbed up a palm tree and tied on his big chef's apron so that it flapped like a white flag. Then he did his silly dance on the beach, waving his big chef's hat wildly back and forth.

Treacle couldn't do much but run backwards and forwards along the sand, jumping in the air every now and again.

Soon they could see the flag. It was the Jolly Roger. A pirate ship. Mr Pattacake felt a knot of fear in his stomach.

'I suppose any ship is better than none,' he said to Treacle.

Treacle agreed with him. He couldn't wait to get home, and would even be glad to see Naughty Tortie again.

The ship was now near enough for them to see figures on the deck waving their bandanas wildly.

Mr Pattacake put his hat back on his head and rolled up his trouser legs ready to wade out into the sea to meet the little boat the pirates were lowering into the water.

Suddenly there was a shout. On the deck a large figure waved, and above him fluttered the Jolly Roger, its friendly eye sockets twinkling.

It was *The Sea Snake* and its crew of good pirates!

Mr Pattacake smiled happily, picked up Treacle, and together they waded out to meet the boat.